This book belongs to

....

Written by Rosie Greening

Illustrated by Stuart Lynch

Jingle Bells

Rosie Greening * Stuart Lynch

make
believe
ideas

Young Jingle was a little horse

who pulled a wooden sleigh.

When winter came, he'd take his friends

for snowy rides each day!

At Christmas time, the horses rushed
to be the first in line,

then made their way to choose a sleigh

that looked simply divine.

But Jingle was
the youngest horse;
he had to wait 'til last.
So he would get
a plain, old sleigh
that wasn't very fast.

"This isn't fair!" young Jingle cried.

"I want to look the best.

I need a glitzy, golden sleigh

that's brighter than the rest!"

So Jingle galloped to a shop
called Glitter, Gold and More.
He bought so many sparkly things,
he emptied out the store!

When **Jingle** went to join his friends,
they **gasped** and gave a **yell**,

for Jingle's sleigh was piled sky-high with giant, golden bells!

The problem was, the heavy bells just weighed poor Jingle down. "I can't quite seem to move my hooves!" he pondered with a frown.

So Jingle's friends all helped to pull

the sleigh along the track.

But Jingle didn't help his friends –

he just sat in the back!

"This **can't** go on," cried Jingle's friends.

"These bells have got to **go!**"

So while he **slept,** they **hid** his bells

beneath the winter **snow.**

When little **Jingle** woke, he found
his precious sleigh was **bare**.

The gold and glitz had disappeared and **not one bell** was there!

So **Jingle** set off through the snow in search of something **bright** to decorate the **empty** sleigh and make it look just **right**.

The **first** things little **Jingle** tried
were **apples** from a tree.

They hung like **bells**, but soon turned **brown** –
attracting **swarms** of bees!

Then Jingle tried some icicles –
the brightest he could find!

But soon they melted, leaving just
a soggy sleigh behind!

With no more sparkly things to try,

he went home in distress.

Poor Jingle looked so miserable,

his friends had to confess . . .

"We're SORRY that we took your bells.

We just want you to know

that it doesn't really matter

if your sleigh has got no glow!"

They led their friend back through the trees
and what a **sight** was there –

they'd **stripped** their sleighs of all the **glitz**,

so every one was **bare**!

And then, with plain but matching sleighs,

they set off through the snow.

Young Jingle went with head held high;

his happy face aglow.

Although poor Jingle's empty sleigh
now looked just like the rest,
he liked to have fun with his friends
much more than looking best!

As Christmas dawned, he saw a glint
of gold under the snow.
And in a flash, young Jingle knew
just where his glitz should go . . .

He shared the **bells** with all his **friends**

so **every** horse's sleigh

would have some **jingle** of its own,

each year on Christmas Day!